REMY
A DOG FROM MAINE

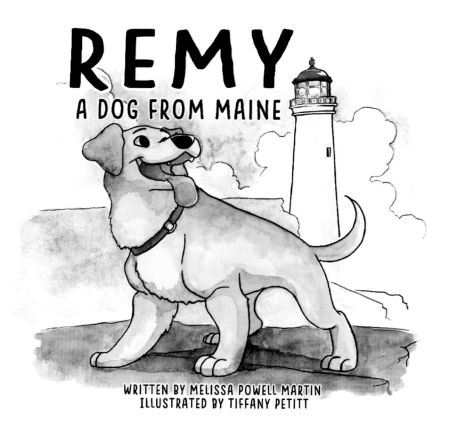

WRITTEN BY MELISSA POWELL MARTIN
ILLUSTRATED BY TIFFANY PETITT

ISBN-10:1987765206
ISBN-13: 978-1987765205

Cover by Tiffany Petitt

DEDICATION

To my three amazing grandbabies.   Aubrey Jean, Eli Warren and Abraham Charles you are so special to me, Mimi loves you to the moon and back!

ACKNOWLEDGEMENT

I want to thank my kids, Nate and Dana for always supporting me and being by my side. I love you both more than you will ever know. My sister Janet for being by my side for my whole life, encouraging me and making me think I can do anything.   Lastly my husband, Jim, what can I say other than Thank you for everything! You always made me feel like this book would happen even through all the delays and frustration. Also thank you for raising Remy to be a wimp giving me the basis for this book! I love you more than you will ever know!

Hi, my name is Remy! I am a big not so brave dog and I live on a lake in the woods of Maine.

There are a lot of scary things in the woods around our house, bears, coyotes, fox, squirrels, chipmunks and once in a while a cat shows up!

My Dad thinks it's funny that I am not very brave, but I know he loves me because he pats me and tells me I am handsome.

I love my Dad more than anything in the world. I want to be with him all the time. He protects me from all the things that scare me, loud noises, and chipmunks, leaves blowing across our yard, and jumping off the dock into the lake.

When my Dad leaves me home it makes me sad and I cry A LOT! I like to sleep in the chair and dream about being brave.

In my dreams I wear a cape which helps me be brave. At first the cape scared me because when it moved I thought something was trying to get me.

Then one day I realized the cape made me into
SUPER REMY!!!

When the delivery man comes to deliver a package I bark instead of hiding behind my friends.

When I wear my cape I run down the dock and jump off the end right into the lake instead of sitting on shore watching my friends jump and chase sticks.

When I wear my cape and my Dad leaves me home I watch our house and keep it safe. I bark to scare away the other animals like bear, fox and coyotes. Even the birds stay up in the trees!

With the cape on I can run fast and chase the squirrels and chipmunks right up a tree. Even the cats don't scare me, I just chase them away. When the leaves blow across the yard I jump on them!

When I wear my cape I am not afraid of anything! I can see myself without the cape being brave as well! I can keep watch and protect my family from any danger that comes along. Nothing scares Super Remy!

Then I hear my Dad's truck coming down our camp road towards our house. I wake up and realize I don't need to be Super Remy anymore!

I don't need the cape because my Dad is home and he will keep me safe and protect me from all the scary things!

This is Remy, he really does love his Dad more than anything in the world and wants to be with him all the time!

Made in the USA
Lexington, KY
19 September 2018